Friends,
No Matter What

Rose Bevins

Perfection Learning®

Illustration: Sue F. Cornelison
Design: Tobi Cunningham

Dedication

This book is dedicated, with love, to
Jessica Lynn Bevins
1977–1993.

About the Author

Rose Bevins is a former high school English teacher. After leaving teaching, she became an editor for an educational publishing company. Six years later, she left to become a freelance editor and writer, and that is what she does today.

Rose has always had a special place in her heart for people with disabilities. "People with disabilities are more like nondisabled people than they are different," she says. She thinks it's important to look at people's abilities, rather than their disabilities.

Rose lives on 30 acres with her husband, son, three dogs, and two cats. In her spare time, she likes to weave, garden, and read.

For information, contact
Perfection Learning® Corporation, 1000 North Second Avenue,
P.O. Box 500, Logan, Iowa 51546-0500.
perfectionlearning.com
Tel: 1-800-831-4190 • Fax: 1-800-543-2745

Paperback ISBN 0-7891-5560-5
Cover Craft® ISBN 0-7569-0644-x

Contents

chapter 1

"**J**ust one more, Kelly. Then I'll be on my way," Mrs. Fields said.

"Sure thing," the boy said. He lifted the box marked "Odds and Ends" for the elderly lady. Then he carried it outside into the summer sun.

Kelly squeezed the box into the back of the little red station wagon. He firmly closed the hatch.

"Thank you so much, dear," said Mrs. Fields. She pulled the front door shut behind her and locked it. Then she came down the front steps.

"I only had a few things left," she said. "And I didn't want to send them in the moving van. I don't think I could have done it without your help."

"You're welcome," the boy said, smiling.

Kelly had lived next door to Mrs. Fields since he was a baby. When he was small, she had often taken care of him when his parents went out. And when he got older, he took care of her.

In the summer, Kelly helped Mrs. Fields with her yard work. In the winter, he shoveled snow for her.

Over the years, Kelly had grown to love this little white-haired lady. He remembered how her kitchen always smelled of cinnamon. And now he was sad to see her go.

"You know, Kelly," Mrs. Fields said. "I'm looking forward to moving to Arizona. I'll be closer to my grandchildren. But I'm sure going to miss you. You've been such a good neighbor."

"I'll miss you too," Kelly said. "But

you'll come back and visit, won't you?"

"Of course I will," said the elderly woman, smiling. "I still have many friends in this town.

"Oh, Kelly, speaking of friends. I almost forgot. The people who bought my house have a son. He's a young man just your age."

Kelly's heart leaped. A boy his age was moving into the neighborhood! The only other one had been Matt Stiles. And he had moved away the year before.

"When are they moving in?" Kelly asked.

"I think they said this Wednesday," the woman said. She opened her car door. "Well, Kelly, it's time to be on my way. Come give me a hug, dear."

Kelly hugged his old friend tightly. "Good-bye, Mrs. Fields," he said. "Take care of yourself. And drive carefully to Arizona."

Mrs. Fields climbed into her car and closed the door. Then she rolled down her window.

"I will, dear," she said. "And you take care of yourself too."

Kelly watched as the car, loaded with boxes, crept out of the driveway.

"And have fun with your new neighbor!" Mrs. Fields called out the window. "I'll bet you two are going to be good friends!"

She waved good-bye as the little red car left the driveway. Then Mrs. Fields slowly headed down the street. Kelly waved until the car turned the corner and was out of sight.

Kelly felt sad. Over the years, he and Mrs. Fields had become good friends. He knew he would miss the spry older woman. But in spite of his sadness, he found himself looking forward to Wednesday.

As he headed home, Kelly thought about his new neighbor. What would he be like? he wondered. Would they have some of the same interests—bike riding, swimming, basketball?

Kelly's favorite sport was basketball. How much fun it would be to have someone right next door to shoot baskets with every day!

If that was the case, Mrs. Fields might be right. He and this new boy might become very good friends.

Wednesday finally came. Kelly ate a quick breakfast. Then he hurried outside.

He spent the rest of the morning shooting baskets. And he kept an eye on the house next door. He didn't want to miss the arrival of the new family.

About 11:00, a huge moving van pulled up to the curb. The movers began unloading furniture and carrying it into the house.

Kelly watched them work. He tried to guess which pieces belonged in the new boy's room.

Kelly saw the men carry in a couch and two big, overstuffed chairs. He figured those were for the living room.

The men took in a dinette set. It would go in the kitchen.

Next they carried in a washer and dryer. Kelly knew those would go in the basement. That's where Mrs. Fields had done her laundry.

Then, to Kelly's surprise, one of the workers pulled a baby crib from the van.

Gee, I never thought about living next door to a baby, Kelly said to himself. It might be fun.

Next the men brought out a fancy white bedroom set. The dresser had curvy legs. And the bed's headboard was trimmed in gold.

Kelly had seen furniture just like that in his cousin Jill's bedroom. He wondered if the new boy had a sister.

Finally, the movers unloaded a matching headboard, dresser, and desk. They were all dark brown wood. And they looked a bit worn.

I'll bet that's for his bedroom, Kelly thought. It looks a lot like mine.

Kelly was tiring of the guessing game. Just then, a shiny blue van backed into the driveway. Kelly felt his heart beat faster. This must be the family! He could hardly wait to get a look at the new boy.

Kelly watched a tall man with dark hair climb out of the driver's seat. The man quickly walked around to the side of the van that was facing Kelly.

The man opened the sliding door. Next he opened the back door of the van and took out a long board. He carried the board around the van. Then he set it on the ground against the side-door opening.

Kelly was puzzled. Looks like a ramp or something, he thought.

"Okay, Jessica," Kelly heard the man say. "You first."

A blond, curly-haired girl came skipping down the ramp. She carried a doll in one arm and a book in the other. Kelly thought she looked about five years old.

At the same time, a woman got out of the front seat. She had taken the baby from the carseat and was holding him.

"Alex, you're next," the man said, smiling into the van. Kelly waited eagerly for the boy to come out.

What would he look like? Kelly wondered. Would he have dark hair like his father? Or blond hair like the little girl? Would he be tall for his age like Kelly?

Kelly held his breath. He waited to catch a glimpse of his new neighbor.

But the next things to appear at the top of the ramp were two large wheels with shiny spokes. Peering into the opening, Kelly could see a pair of sneakers between the wheels. He realized with surprise that he was looking at someone sitting in a wheelchair.

The chair slowly appeared from the darkness of the van. With a look of concentration, a young boy used his hands to carefully guide the wheels of the chair down the ramp.

"Come on, Alex," the woman said, smiling. "Let's go see our new house."

The boy's family waited until he was

safe on the driveway. Then they all
headed up the front sidewalk toward the
door of their new home.

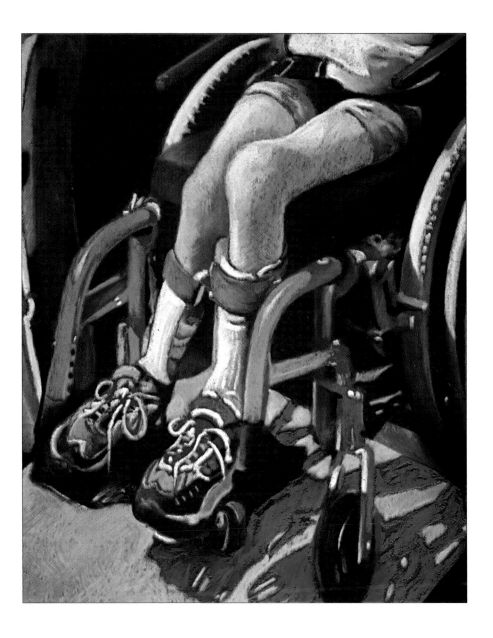

As Kelly looked on in amazement, the boy glanced his way. Then he smiled at Kelly. Not knowing why, Kelly dropped the basketball and ran into his own house.

3

Kelly was quiet at dinner that evening.

"You're hardly eating a thing," his mother said. "Are you feeling all right, Kelly?"

Kelly shrugged his shoulders. "Yeah, I'm okay."

He tried another bite of spaghetti. It was usually his favorite dish. But for some reason, it didn't taste very good that night.

"Is something bothering you?" asked Mrs. Carlson.

Kelly shrugged again.

"Do you miss your father?" Mrs. Carlson asked.

Kelly's father was a salesman. He was often out of town during the week.

"No, I'm all right," the boy answered without looking up. "Mom, may I be excused?"

Mrs. Carlson looked at him with concern. "Well, I suppose so," she said. "But I'm really surprised to see you eat so little of your favorite meal. That's not like you."

"It was good, Mom. But I'm just not hungry," Kelly replied. "I'll be outside shooting baskets." He headed out the door.

Kelly shot baskets for a while. Usually he made most of his shots. But that night, he missed more than he made.

Mrs. Carlson came out a few minutes later. She sat on the deck and watched Kelly.

"You know, I'd like to help if something is bothering you," she finally said.

Kelly stopped dribbling the ball for a

moment. "Mom, why are some people in wheelchairs?" he asked.

Mrs. Carlson looked surprised at this question. "People are usually in wheelchairs because they have a physical disability," she replied.

"What exactly is a *physical disability*?" Kelly asked. He'd heard the term many times. But it was still a mystery to him.

"It's something that keeps your body from working the way it should," his mother explained.

The boy frowned. "But what causes a physical disability, Mom?"

"Well, either a person is born with a disability. Or it's caused by an illness or an accident," Mrs. Carlson answered.

Kelly was quiet for a moment. Then he shot one last basket and joined his mother on the deck.

"Can a person catch a physical disability from another person?" he asked, sitting down in the lawn chair next to his mother's.

Mrs. Carlson smiled. "No, Kelly," she said. "Disabilities aren't catching. But why are you asking all of these questions?"

Kelly avoided his mother's eyes. "Well—I was outside today when the new people moved in next door," he said.

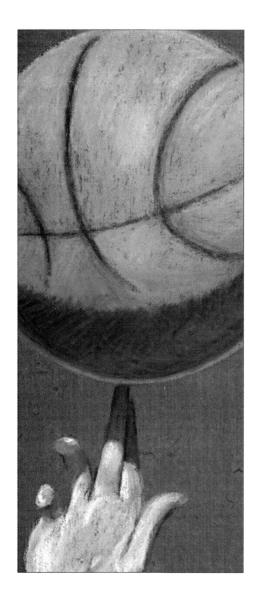

"And?" Mrs. Carlson asked, inviting him to go on.

Kelly spun the ball on the tip of his finger for a few seconds. Finally he spoke. "You know the boy Mrs. Fields told me about?"

"The new boy next door?" his mother replied.

"Yeah," Kelly said. "Anyway, he's in a wheelchair."

"Oh, I see," said Mrs. Carlson. "Well, did you go over and meet him?"

Kelly bounced the ball on the deck a few times. Then, without looking up, he said, "No, I ran into the house. I don't know why. I think I was kind of scared."

Mrs. Carlson laid her hand on Kelly's shoulder. "I'm sure there's nothing to be afraid of," she said gently. "A person in a

wheelchair is just a person who needs help getting around. Maybe if you got to know this boy, you'd like him."

Kelly looked up sadly. "But, Mom, I wanted a friend to play basketball with. And he's in a wheelchair."

"Is that what's bothering you, Kelly? That you don't have someone to play basketball with?" his mother asked.

Kelly looked down again. "I guess so," he said.

"Kelly, you know we aren't all able to do the same things. Even if we don't have disabilities," Mrs. Carlson reminded him. "Remember Matt? He couldn't swim, could he? But you can swim like a fish. Did that keep the two of you from becoming friends?"

"Of course not," Kelly said.

"That's because you didn't base your friendship on swimming, did you?"

Kelly shook his head.

"And you shouldn't base a friendship on basketball," Mrs. Carlson said. "Friendships should be based on liking other people for who they are. And then accepting them for what they can or can't do. You might consider giving the boy next door a chance."

Kelly shrugged his shoulders.

"Well, think about it," Mrs. Carlson said. "Tomorrow I plan to take over a casserole to welcome the family to the neighborhood. It might be a good time for you to come along and meet this boy."

"I don't know, Mom," Kelly replied.

"Well, as I said, think about it," Mrs. Carlson said, standing up. "Maybe after a good night's rest, you'll feel different about all of this tomorrow. Why don't we go in now? It's getting late. The mosquitoes will be coming out soon."

Kelly sighed.

"Okay," he said. He went into the

garage and put his ball away. As he headed toward his house, he glanced next door. No one was outside. But he could see lights shining in most of the windows.

They're probably unpacking, he thought. Then he went into the house.

As Kelly lay in bed that night he thought about the boy next door. What would it be like to have a friend who couldn't walk? he wondered. What kinds of things could they do together? Could he have fun with someone who couldn't run, jump, or ride a bike the way he did? Could he possibly have fun with someone who couldn't play basketball?

The next morning, Mrs. Carlson baked a tuna-noodle casserole to take next door.

She slipped on her oven mitts and picked up the hot dish. "Are you ready to meet the new family?" she asked Kelly.

"I guess so, " Kelly replied. He followed her out the door. But he wasn't at all sure that he was ready.

Together they climbed the porch steps of Mrs. Fields' old house. Kelly rang the bell because his mother's hands were full.

A woman opened the door. Kelly recognized her as the woman who had been carrying the baby the day before. She smiled at Kelly and his mother.

"Hello," Mrs. Carlson said. "I'm Patsy Carlson. And this is my son, Kelly. We live next door."

"How do you do?" said the woman. "I'm Connie Miller. Won't you come in?"

"Thank you," Mrs. Carlson said, entering the house with Kelly. "We brought this casserole to welcome you to the neighborhood."

"Oh, how thoughtful," Mrs. Miller said. "Thank you so much."

She nodded toward the stacks of boxes in the living room. "You'll have to excuse the mess. We still have so much unpacking to do." She led them into the kitchen. "You can just set it on top of the stove, Patsy."

"I know how much work unpacking is," said Mrs. Carlson, setting the dish down. "Maybe this will keep you from having to stop and make lunch today."

"It smells delicious," Mrs. Miller said. "Can I get you something to drink? I've just made some lemonade for the kids."

"Yes, thank you," Kelly's mother replied.

"Kelly, would you like some lemonade?" asked Mrs. Miller.

"No, thank you," Kelly said politely.

Mrs. Miller poured a glass of lemonade for Kelly's mother. Then she asked, "How old are you, Kelly?"

"Twelve," he replied.

"Really? My son, Alex, is just your age. Would you like to meet him? He's in his room unpacking some of his things."

Kelly looked at his mother. She nodded her head.

"Okay," he said. He turned to follow Mrs. Miller down the hall.

They passed a room on the right. Kelly glanced in. He saw a little girl sitting on the floor among a mountain of boxes. He recognized her as the girl who had come skipping down the ramp the day before.

Mrs. Miller paused in the doorway. "This is my daughter, Jessica."

"Hi," Jessica said, smiling.

"Hello," Kelly answered.

"Jessica, this is Kelly Carlson," Mrs. Miller said. "He's one of our neighbors."

"I'm unpacking my dolls," Jessica said brightly. She held one up for him to see.

"That's nice," Kelly said.

The door of the next room was almost closed. As they passed, Mrs. Miller whispered, "This is the baby's room. He's taking a nap."

Looking down the hallway, Kelly could see two silver wheels just inside the next doorway. Suddenly, the uneasy feeling from the day before returned.

Kelly followed Mrs. Miller into the room, glancing at the empty chair as they passed.

"Alex, someone is here to meet you," Mrs. Miller said. "This is Kelly Carlson. He lives next door."

The boy Kelly had seen the day before was sitting on his bed. He was unpacking what looked like a collection of rocks. Several were spread out before him on the bed.

Alex looked up and smiled slightly. "Hello," he said shyly.

"Hi," Kelly answered, just as shyly.

"I see you're unpacking your rock collection, Alex," said Mrs. Miller. "I should have known you'd unpack that right away. I'll leave you two boys alone to get to know each other. Kelly, let me know if you change your mind about that lemonade."

"I will," Kelly said. He watched her leave the room and wished he could follow.

After Mrs. Miller had gone, the boys spent a few seconds in silence. Kelly glanced around the room. Again, his eyes rested on the wheelchair.

"Do you want to sit down?" Alex asked.

Kelly shrugged. "Sure," he said. He sat on the edge of the bed and looked at Alex. His head and arms looked fine. But his feet were small for a boy his age. And his legs looked very thin.

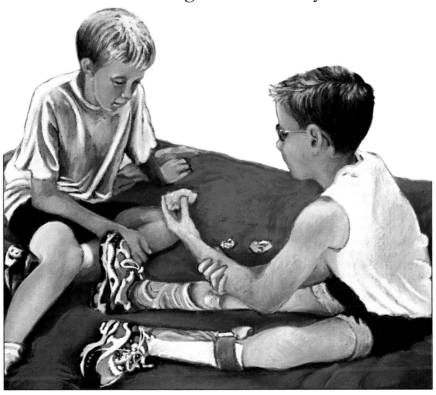

Mrs. Carlson had said that Alex probably had a physical disability. Kelly wondered to himself what Alex's disability was. His gaze returned to the chair. It looked so cold and shiny sitting there with its two big wheels. Kelly had a hard time taking his eyes off it.

Alex must have noticed. "That's my wheelchair," he said. "I use it to get around."

"Oh," Kelly said.

"I can't walk," Alex added quietly but matter-of-factly.

For a few seconds, neither of the boys spoke. Then Kelly asked, "Do you have a—physical disability?"

Alex looked a little surprised. But he smiled and answered. "Yes, my legs don't work very well," he said.

"Why?" Kelly asked quietly.

"I have spina bifida," Alex replied. "I've never been able to walk."

"What's spina bif—" Kelly began.

Alex smiled. "Bifida," he said. "It means I have a problem with my backbone. My spine."

"Oh." Kelly wanted to know what kind of problem. But he didn't know if he should ask any more questions. He was relieved when Alex asked, "Hey, do you like rocks?"

Kelly shrugged again. "I don't know much about them," he said.

"I'm crazy about them," said Alex. "In fact, I'm going to be a geologist when I grow up. That's someone who studies rocks."

"I know," Kelly said. He had learned that word in science class.

"I have a whole collection," Alex went on, pointing to the box beside him on the bed. "Want to help me unpack them?"

"I guess," Kelly said.

Alex reached into the box on the bed. He handed Kelly a wad of scrunched up newspapers.

"Go ahead. Unwrap it," he said. "See which one you got."

Kelly unwrapped an orange rock about the size of an egg. Its surface was rough to the touch and sparkly.

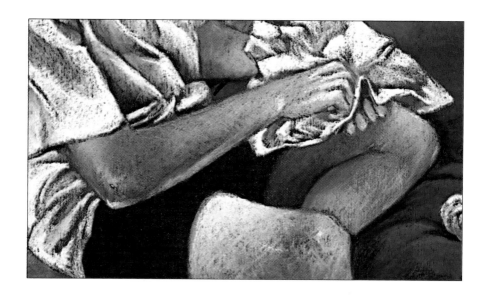

"That's sandstone," Alex said. "See the ripple marks on it? That means it was formed in water. You can even tell which way the water was flowing by looking at the ripples."

"Why does it sparkle?" Kelly asked.

"It has quartz in it," Alex replied. He picked up one of the rocks in front of him. "This is quartz," he said, handing it to Kelly.

Kelly studied the quartz with interest. It had six sides and was pointed on each end. And it was so clear. He could see through it.

"This is a rock?" Kelly asked. "It looks like a diamond."

Alex laughed. "Actually quartz is a mineral," he explained. "Rocks are made of minerals."

"Oh, yeah, I remember that now from science class," Kelly said. "But I can't remember—is a diamond a mineral?"

"Well, sort of," Alex said. "A diamond is a gem. When minerals have a lot of pressure and heat put on them, they become gems."

Kelly was surprised at how much Alex knew. "Can I unwrap another?" he asked.

"Sure, go ahead," Alex replied.

The next one Kelly unwrapped was purple. "What's this?"

"That's quartz too," Alex said.

"Why is it purple?" Kelly asked.

"Because it has iron in it," Alex replied.

"Oh," Kelly said, nodding his head.

One by one the boys unwrapped the rocks. They placed them on a shelf above Alex's bed.

When they were finished, Alex said, "Hey, do you want to see a picture of the largest diamond in the world?"

"Okay," Kelly said.

"It's called the Hope Diamond," Alex explained. "It's kept in a museum in Washington, D.C. We went there last summer. I took a picture of it."

"Where's the picture?" Kelly asked.

"I think it's in the closet," Alex replied. He lowered himself off the edge of the bed. "I'll look."

Kelly watched in amazement as Alex pulled himself across the room with his arms. His legs trailed out behind him.

"Here it is," Alex announced. He took a picture album out of a box on the floor of the closet.

Kelly crossed the room for a better look. On the way, he glanced into the closet.

Hanging just inside the door was a shiny yellow uniform. It had the number *8* and the word *TIGERS* written in bold, black lettering on it. He looked at Alex. "Is that—a basketball uniform?" he asked.

"Yeah," replied Alex, thumbing through the book.

"Um—whose is it?" asked Kelly.

Alex looked up. "It's mine," he said. "I'm on a team."

"You play basketball?" Kelly asked. He tried to keep from sounding too surprised.

"Sure. I play in a summer league for kids in wheelchairs. We play every week at the youth center downtown," Alex explained.

Kelly frowned. "I don't understand," he said. "You play basketball sitting down?"

"Oh, yeah," Alex replied. "And we've got a great coach. Mr. Cumings. He's in a wheelchair too. He taught us how to dribble the ball to the side of the chair. And how to shoot from a sitting position."

Kelly was about to ask Alex more. But

his mother and Mrs. Miller appeared in the doorway.

"My, it looks as if you boys have been busy. Nice work," Mrs. Miller said. "Alex, this is Mrs. Carlson, Kelly's mother."

"Hi," Alex said.

"Hello, Alex. I'm very glad to meet you," Mrs. Carlson said, smiling. "Kelly, I'm afraid it's time to go. We've got some errands to run before lunch."

"Okay," Kelly said. "Good-bye, Alex. Thanks for letting me see your rock collection."

"Bye, Kelly," Alex said. "Thanks for helping me. Hey, come again some time. Then you can look at the picture."

"Um—yeah, maybe," Kelly said. As he turned to leave he spotted the chair by the door again. It certainly didn't look to him like anything you could play basketball in.

chapter 5

A few days later, Kelly headed out to shoot baskets. After a few minutes, he heard the pounding of a hammer. He looked toward the Millers' house and saw a man working by the front door. Alex was sitting in his chair on the lawn watching. The big wheels gleamed in the sunlight. Kelly couldn't help noticing how small Alex looked compared to the chair.

"Hi, Kelly," Alex called when he spied him.

"Hi," Kelly said. He headed into the Millers' yard, still carrying his basketball.

"This is my dad," Alex said. "He's building a ramp for my chair. It's so I can get in and out of the house more easily."

"Hello, Kelly," Mr. Miller said, shaking Kelly's hand. He glanced at the basketball Kelly was holding. "I see you like basketball."

"Yeah, I do," Kelly said.

"Well, you two have something in common then," Alex's father said. "Alex is quite a fan himself."

"Hey, do you want to shoot some hoops?" Alex asked brightly.

Kelly shrugged. "I don't know," he said. He was still wondering how Alex could possibly shoot baskets from his wheelchair. And he was afraid he would hurt Alex's feelings if he outplayed him.

But Alex had already started down the driveway. "Come on, let's go," he called over his shoulder. Kelly watched as Alex worked his chair across the concrete.

"Have fun," called Mr. Miller, returning to his work.

Kelly caught up with Alex. But he felt kind of funny walking beside him as they headed toward the basketball hoop.

The difference in their heights bothered Kelly. Alex's head barely came up to his waist. And Kelly was afraid to walk too close to the chair for fear of getting run over by its big wheels. But he also noticed how skillfully Alex wheeled the chair onto the sidewalk and then up the Carlsons' sloped driveway.

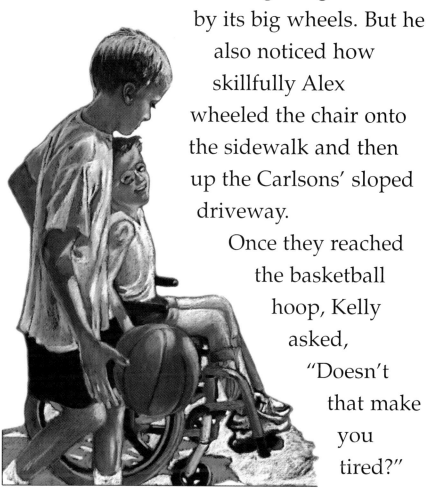

Once they reached the basketball hoop, Kelly asked, "Doesn't that make you tired?"

"What?" Alex said.

"Wheeling yourself around," Kelly said. "It looks like hard work."

Alex shrugged. "Sometimes it is," he admitted. "But I'm pretty used to it. And I work out with weights to make my arms stronger. Dad says that's why I'm a pretty good shot. Are you ready to play?"

"I guess," answered Kelly as he handed the ball to Alex. "Here. You can go first."

Alex took the ball and backed up his chair. Then he dribbled the ball twice to the side, aimed carefully, and shot. The ball hit the rim and bounced back onto the driveway.

Kelly was surprised at how fast Alex moved next. He swerved his chair, snatched up the ball, and shot again. This time the ball teetered on the rim. Then it dropped back down to the driveway.

Alex smiled and tossed the ball to

Kelly. "This hoop is a little higher than the one we use for our games," he said. "Guess it'll take some getting used to. Your shot."

Kelly dribbled the ball a few times, aimed, and shot. The ball hit the backboard and bounced right back to him. He shot again and missed again.

"Try shooting more with your fingertips," Alex said.

Kelly aimed carefully. This time he placed the ball more on his fingertips than on his hand. The ball easily dropped through the net.

"Hey, thanks," he said. "Nobody ever told me that before."

"No problem," Alex said. "It's just something we learned from Coach Cumings."

The boys spent the next hour shooting baskets. Kelly made a lot of his shots. Alex made one once in a while. But he didn't seem to get discouraged.

"This is going to take some practice," Alex said. "But if I can get better at this height, just think how good I'll be in our games."

"Yeah," Kelly said, shooting again and

making it. He tossed the ball to Alex.

"Hey, we've got a game this Saturday," Alex said. He took a shot and made it. Then he tossed the ball to Kelly. "You can come watch it. That is, if you want to."

"I don't know," Kelly replied. He wasn't sure he'd enjoy watching a wheelchair basketball game. He thought it might be pretty boring. "My dad will be back by then. And we might have other plans."

Just then Alex's father called him for lunch.

"Well, okay, it's up to you. Gotta go," said Alex. "See you later."

Kelly watched as Alex turned his chair around and wheeled down the driveway. All he could see from where he was standing was Alex's head sticking up above the back of the seat and his arms straining to hold the chair back on the slope.

Once again, Kelly thought how small Alex looked compared to the chair. From where Kelly stood, it looked as if the chair had swallowed the boy and was carrying him away.

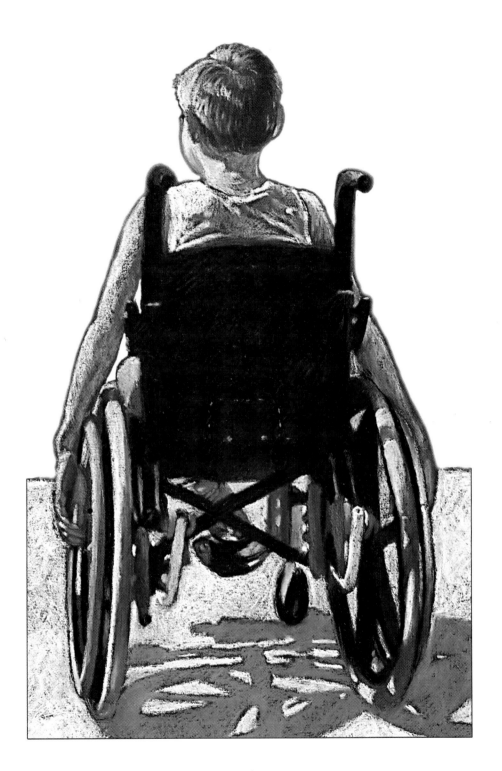

On Friday, Kelly's father got home. The whole family went out for pizza. During dinner, Mrs. Carlson told Kelly's father about the new family next door.

"Their son is Kelly's age," she added.

"Really? Have you met him yet, Kel?" Mr. Carlson asked with interest.

"Yeah," Kelly answered. He reached for another piece of pizza. "His name is Alex."

"Well, what do you think of him?" his father asked.

Kelly shrugged. "He's okay. He's got a rock collection."

"You don't sound as thrilled as I thought you would to have a boy your age next door. Is there a problem?" asked Mr. Carlson.

"Just that he's in a wheelchair," Kelly said.

"Oh," Mr. Carlson said. "Is that a problem?"

Kelly shrugged his shoulders. "It's just not the way I thought it would be," he said.

Kelly's mother mentioned the basketball game that Alex had invited Kelly to.

"Hey, I think that sounds great," said Mr. Carlson. "I've never seen wheelchair basketball. It might be kind of interesting. Want to go, son?"

"I don't know, Dad," Kelly said. "Maybe it'd be interesting. But it might be kind of boring too."

"Well, I think we should at least give it a try," his father said. "After all, Alex did invite you. It would be rude not to go if we have no other plans."

"Yeah," Kelly mumbled. "I guess so." He took a big bite of pizza. He hoped his dad wouldn't ask him any more questions if his mouth was full.

Saturday morning, Kelly and his dad drove to the youth center. The first thing Kelly noticed was the number of vans parked in the spaces reserved for people with disabilities.

Entering the center, Kelly saw more wheelchairs than he had ever seen before. The whole gym seemed to be filled with silver wheels and shiny handles.

Kelly and his dad took a seat in the bleachers behind the Tigers' bench. Kelly noticed that the other team was called the Cardinals.

The two teams were gathered on the sidelines. The coaches were also in wheelchairs. They were quietly giving players last-minute tips before the game began.

Kelly searched the Tigers' team for Alex. But he could only see the backs of the heads of most of the players. He didn't spot Alex until the buzzer sounded and the starting players wheeled out onto the floor. Then he saw Alex, tensely leaning forward in his chair. The referee blew her whistle. Suddenly, ten chairs were in motion.

Alex's team had possession of the ball. A boy with number 16 on his uniform headed down the floor. He skillfully dribbled the ball alongside his chair. As he neared the basket, he passed the ball to number 12 who was waiting at the baseline.

Number 12 drove toward the basket. He was cut off by a Cardinal. Quickly he turned his chair and passed off to a teammate in the lane.

That player banked the ball off the backboard. It slid through the basket for the first two points of the game. The crowd around Kelly and his father cheered.

The referee picked up the ball and handed it to a Cardinal. When the ref blew her whistle, the Cardinal inbounded it to a teammate. Suddenly, the fleet of chairs wheeled to the other end of the court.

Kelly watched as the Cardinals passed the ball from player to player. He was amazed at how quickly the boys in the chairs moved.

Other than the height of the basket, Kelly could only see one difference between the rules of wheelchair basketball and the kind he played. Instead of being allowed two steps for every dribble, each player was allowed two pushes of his chair.

Sometimes play was interrupted by the collision of two chairs. This was usually followed by the ref's whistle and the calling of a foul.

By halftime the score was 22–20. The Cardinals were in the lead.

As the players left the court, Alex spotted Kelly in the crowd and waved. Kelly waved back.

"Pretty good game, huh, Kel?" asked Mr. Carlson.

"Yeah, it's okay," Kelly said.

"Want some popcorn?" his father asked.

"Sure," Kelly said.

"I'll buy, you fly," Mr. Carlson said. He dug in his pockets for some change.

Kelly got back with the popcorn just as the second half was beginning.

In the first minute, Alex's team made a basket. The score was tied. Then the Cardinals sank one. Then the Tigers hit again. The lead went back and forth for the rest of the second half. With less than a minute left, the Tigers led by a single point.

The people around Kelly were up on their feet, cheering the Tigers on. Kelly found himself doing the same. He realized that he was as excited as he'd ever been at a basketball game.

A Cardinal inbounded the ball to a teammate. But the pass was high. The ball bounced down the court. Alex and a Cardinal player headed for the ball.

In the scramble, their chairs collided. The referee's whistle screeched. She called a foul on Alex for blocking the Cardinal. The player in red headed for the free throw line.

With a look of concentration, the Cardinal bounced the ball to the side twice. Then he took aim and shot. The free throw was good. And the score was tied 38–38. Only 20 seconds remained in the game.

The Tigers' coach signaled for a time-out. Both teams headed for the sidelines. Alex's team huddled around Coach Cumings as he spoke to them.

"What do you think the coach is saying?" Kelly asked his father.

"He's probably telling them to get the ball down court and into the hands of number 12 as fast as they can," Mr. Carlson said. "Looks like Number 12 is their best shooter."

A minute later, the teams headed back onto the court. Kelly watched as the Tigers took up their planned positions.

The ball was inbounded. Then it was quickly passed among the players to the other end of the court. There, number 12 was waiting to make the final shot of the game.

As the other players headed down the court, number 12 snatched up the ball, turned his chair, and shot. The shot was short. It hit the rim and bounced unexpectedly into Alex's lap.

Kelly saw a look of surprise cross Alex's face. Then he picked up the ball, positioned it on his fingertips, and shot. The ball dropped neatly through the net. The crowd cheered wildly. The Tigers had won 40–38!

"Wow! That was a good game, Dad," Kelly said.

"It sure was," Mr. Carlson replied. "I'm glad we came."

"Me too," Kelly said.

They stood up then and started to make their way down the bleachers. When they reached the floor, Kelly saw Alex headed their way.

"So what did you think of the game, Kelly?" Alex asked, flushed and smiling.

"It was great, Alex. And you made the winning basket! Good going!" Kelly said.

"Thanks," Alex said.

"Alex, I'm Kelly's father," Mr. Carlson said, reaching down to shake the boy's hand. "Good game."

"Thanks," Alex said. "Hey, and thanks for coming, Kelly. I'm really glad you did."

Kelly looked at Alex's happy face. He realized that for the first time since they had met, he was seeing Alex as just a boy. Not as a boy with a disability.

"I'm glad I came too," Kelly said. "It was a good game."

"Well, I've got to go," Alex said, turning his chair. "My dad's waiting. We're going out with the team for ice cream. Feel like shooting some hoops later?"

"Sure," Kelly said. "Come on over when you get home."

"Okay, see you then," Alex said.

Alex headed across the gym floor. Mr. Carlson turned to Kelly. He said, "He seems like a nice boy, Kel."

Kelly nodded and said, "He is, Dad."

As they headed to the parking lot, Kelly knew that his mother had been right. It didn't matter that Alex couldn't run, jump, or ride a bike the way he could. And it didn't matter that he didn't play basketball in quite the same way. It also didn't matter that Kelly couldn't rattle off the names of 17 kinds of rocks and minerals. Kelly knew that he and Alex were just like all boys. In some ways they were alike. And in some ways they were different. But they liked each other. And that's what mattered most of all.

Spina Bifida

The central nervous system allows us to move, feel, taste, and see. The spinal cord is an important part of this system. It carries messages from our brains to different parts of our bodies.

Before a baby is born, the bones of the spine create a column. This column surrounds the spinal cord. It is called the *spinal column*. The spinal column protects the spinal cord just as the skull protects the brain.

Sometimes the spinal column fails to close around the spinal cord. This condition is called *spina bifida*, or "split spine." It results in a gap, or split, in the spine.

The spinal cord is not protected where this split occurs. So it is open to injury. If the spinal cord is injured, messages from the brain don't get through to the body.

Spina bifida is a birth defect. It occurs in 1 out of every 1,000 births. It can be very mild or very serious. The mildest form occurs when only one of the bones around the spine does not form properly. This condition rarely causes problems. Many people don't know they have the condition until it shows up on a routine X-ray.

The most serious form of spina bifida causes paralysis below the waist. Children who have this condition have problems walking. Or they may not be able to walk at all.

Like Alex in the story, they may use a wheelchair. Or they may wear braces on their legs and use crutches or a walker to get around. But this does not stop them from leading active lives.

Young people with spina bifida go swimming and snorkeling. Some, like Alex, play wheelchair basketball. Others go skiing in special kinds of chairs called *bi-skis*. And these kids have the same interests as others their age: video games, music, movies, clothes, and computers.

Here are some very successful people who have spina bifida.

John Mellencamp—Grammy Award-winning musician

Jean Driscoll—Seven-time winner of the Boston Marathon and silver medalist at the 1992 and 1996 Olympics

Jay Bradford Fowler—Author of 17
books of poetry

Jim LeBrecht—Sound designer and
co-author of *Sound and
Music for the Theatre: The
Art of Technique and Design.*
Five-time winner of the
San Francisco Bay Area
Drama Critics' Circle
Award for Outstanding
Sound Design.